Nana's Garden

Sophy Williams

RED FOX

One day in early autumn, Thomas was going out to play.

'You come too, Nana,' he said.

'Me?' said Nana. 'I'm too old to play.'

'I wish you weren't,' said Thomas.

The sun cast shadows in Nana's garden. Thomas kicked up the leaves, still wet from the morning's rain. A branch cracked, an apple fell.

'Who's there?' said Thomas.

The wind in the trees murmured, *'It's only me. An echo, a whisper, a heartbeat.'*

The air grew cold in Nana's garden. Thomas turned and looked around. The long grass was flattened as if someone had been walking there. A trail of footsteps seemed to run in and out of the trees. Thomas followed them, all round the orchard and across the lawn to Nana's shed.

Thomas had never been inside, but now he thought perhaps there was something precious hidden there.

As he reached up to open the door, he thought he saw someone watching him.

'Who's there?' he said.

The wind whistled under the door. *'Inside,'* it said. *'Inside.'*

A pale light shone through the little window, and lit up the muddle inside. Thomas began to search. Through the ancient chest of drawers, behind an old mirror, inside a box of rusty tools. Then at the back of the shed Thomas found a tall cupboard. He opened the door. Dust flew up in a cloud. Spiders and mice scuttled. From a dark corner, a worn, friendly face looked out at him.

Very gently, very carefully, Thomas lifted out the treasure.

At the window, the small fingers of another child gripped the sill. There was a shimmer of blue, a wisp of hair, a bright eye watching.

'There, there,' sang the other child. *'He's been waiting, all these long years.'*

Thomas hugged the treasure and took it outside. As he sat on the damp grass he felt a tap on his shoulder.

'Hello.'

'Hello,' said Thomas. 'Who are you? This is Nana's garden.'

'It's my garden too,' said the other child. *'I've come for Joshua.'*

'But I found him,' said Thomas.

'I know,' she said. *'But he's mine.'*

The wind was very still. Thomas looked at the little girl. 'Let's play,' he said.

They played with Joshua.
They played I-spy and giant's
footsteps. They played statues and
hide-and-seek. The sun came out.

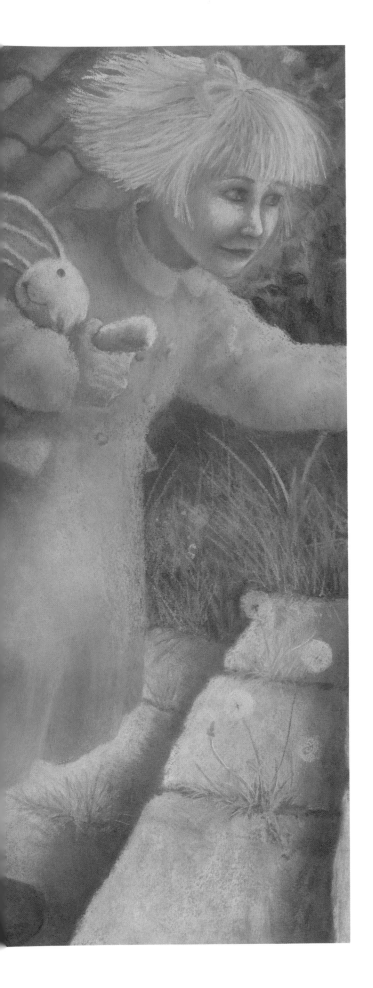

They raced in and out the trees –
all around the orchard and up the
steps.

'*Come on,*' said the other child.
'*I'll show you the secret places.*'

They ran through Nana's garden to the wild part where Thomas had never been before. Brambles caught at their clothes, leaves crunched under their feet.

'Look Thomas,' said the other child. '*This is where Josie and Tsar are buried. Josie was a big sad labrador. Tsar was a snappy little terrier. He pined for days when Josie died. He didn't last long after.*'

'*And see that rose over there,*' said the child. '*I planted it because my name is Rose.*'

'Nana's name is Rose too,' said Thomas.

The light began to fade in Nana's garden.

'*I'm tired now,*' said Rose. '*I've got to go.*'

'Don't go,' said Thomas. 'Stay with me.'

'*I am with you,*' she said. '*I'm always with you.*'

'Please don't go,' said Thomas again.

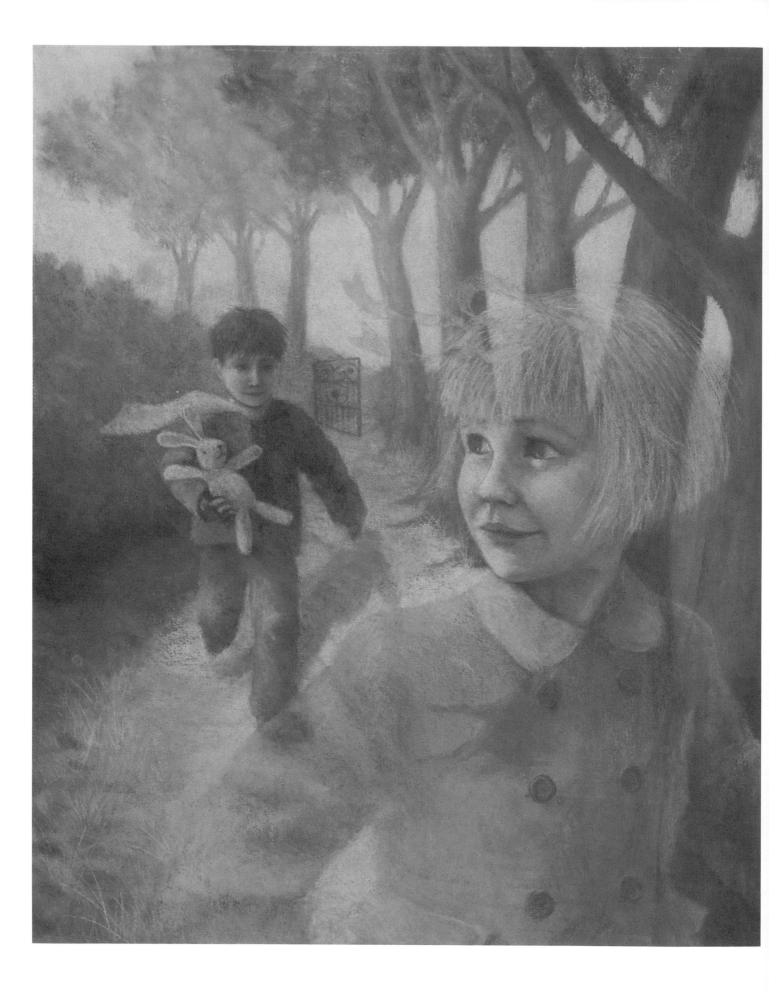

But Rose was already
through the gate.
Thomas ran after her.
'Here, take Joshua,' he
said. 'He's yours.'

Then the light was gone in Nana's garden. There was no one there. Just an echo, a shadow, a heartbeat.

Thomas ran back inside and
hugged his grandmother fiercely.
'I love you, Nana,' he said.

For Poppy, Daniel, Jasmin and Ruthie

A Red Fox Book

Published by Random House Children's Books
20 Vauxhall Bridge Road, London SW1V 2SA

A division of Random House UK Ltd
London Melbourne Sydney Auckland
Johannesburg and agencies throughout the world

Copyright © Sophy Williams 1993

1 3 5 7 9 10 8 6 4 2

First published in Great Britain by
Hutchinson Children's Books 1993

Red Fox edition 1995

Printed and bound in Singapore by Tien Wah Press (Pte) Ltd

RANDOM HOUSE UK Limited Reg. No. 954009

ISBN 0 09 996500 3